THE FISHERMAN AND HIS WIFE

a brand-new version by

Rosemary Wells

pictures by

Eleanor Hubbard

Dial Books for Young Readers ◆ New York

Published by Dial Books for Young Readers
A member of Penguin Putnam Inc.
375 Hudson Street
New York, New York 10014

Designed by Amelia Lau Carling
Printed in Hong Kong
First Edition
1 3 5 7 9 10 8 6 4 2

Library of Congress Cataloging in Publication Data
Wells, Rosemary.
The fisherman and his wife : a brand-new version / by Rosemary Wells;
pictures by Eleanor Hubbard. — 1st ed.
p. cm.
Summary: The fisherman's greedy wife is never satisfied
with the wishes granted her by an enchanted fish.
ISBN 0-8037-1850-0. — ISBN 0-8037-1851-9 (lib.)
[1. Fairy tales. 2. Folklore—Germany.] I. Hubbard, Eleanor, ill.
II. Von dem Fischer und seiner Frau. III. Fisherman and his wife. English. IV. Title.
PZ8.W455Fi 1998 398.2'0943'02—dc20 95-6486 [E] CIP AC

The paintings were prepared with gouache, watercolor, and colored pencil.

To El, Geoff, and Hubs—R.W.

To the memory of my parents,
Mary and Irving Hubbard,
who gave me an uncommonly happy childhood
filled with cats, crayons, and love—E. H.

Once upon a time in the country of Norway there was a fisherman and his wife. They lived very happily in their cottage by the shore of the Torva Fjord. Every morning Ragnar sailed out to fish.

Whether the sun was hot or the wind was cold, Ragnar came home to Ulla, kissed her on the nose, and said, "My dearest, I hope you are as happy as I am in this beautiful world."

Ulla always answered, "Oh, yes, my love. We have everything we want, mountains all around us, and petunias in the window box.

"But mostly we have everything because we have each other."

And so Ulla and Ragnar smiled smiles of love across the candle flames and ate a fragrant dinner of homemade bread, herring, and potatoes with dill sauce.

One day when he was out in the middle of the Torva Fjord, Ragnar felt a huge tug on his line. He pulled in his catch and on his hook was a fish with scales like sapphires, eyes green as emeralds, and ruby red lips. To his great surprise the fish could talk. "Let me off the hook, fisherman, and I'll grant any wish you name!" it burbled.

Ragnar didn't believe a word the fish said. "How about some lobster, then?" he asked. And dozens of lobsters leaped into his net.

Ragnar thanked the fish, unhooked its mouth, and watched the sapphire scales snap back into the deep.

That evening Ragnar was so excited, he forgot to kiss Ulla. He told her about the fish who granted wishes.

Ulla was delighted. But then she said, "Ragnar, we can't eat lobster. Our cooking pot isn't large enough for lobster. Tell the fish we need a bigger pot as well."

The next day while Ragnar was out in his boat, Ulla made a special cloudberry cake. She hummed a sea song to the squawks of the gulls dropping their clams on the rocks outside. At just the moment she iced the cake, there was a knock on the door.

It was a peddler.
"Good morning," said the peddler. "I have something for you!"

The peddler took a huge silver kettle out of his wagon. "Already paid for!" he said. Then he put it by the kitchen door and disappeared down the street.

That night Ulla made lobster thermidor. "Tomorrow," she said, "we'll have lobster salad sandwiches and invite the neighbors in!"

Every night Ragnar brought home more lobster. Ulla used her new silver kettle. Everyone on the street came by for a bite to eat.

At the end of the week Ulla said to Ragnar, "There's no room in our kitchen for this enormous kettle. Why don't you tell the talking fish we need a brand-new house with a bigger kitchen?"

So Ragnar went out and he called the fish. Soon ruby red lips broke the surface of the water. "All right," said the fish. "Go home and the house will be already built."

Sure enough, when Ragnar went home Ulla was standing in the doorway of a bungalow with a porch and two chimneys.

"The peddler came by," said Ulla. "This time he brought a house!"

After a few days Ragnar asked Ulla why she did not look happy in her new home. "It's the neighbors," said Ulla. "They won't talk to me. This is the biggest house on the street and they are all jealous. I think we need to move to a richer neighborhood. Why don't you ask the fish?"

So Ragnar went out in his boat.

Sure enough, that afternoon the peddler came by again. "These are the keys to a mansion on the hill, already paid for," said the peddler.

And so Ragnar and Ulla moved to a mansion with forty rooms on the top of the highest hill in town.

Ulla seemed happy. Ragnar was not.

"I miss the sound of the sea," he said. "I don't like the smell of these Oriental rugs and I don't like the looks of those ancestors in the oil paintings."

"All we need are new friends!" said Ulla. "Let's throw a big party. Everyone will come. That will make the stars shine in your eyes again. Now, I must have a fancy dress with silver dancing shoes. We have to hire an orchestra, cooks to cook, and servants to serve. Go ask the fish, Ragnar."

And so Ragnar went out in his boat and called to the fish again.

In a flash of sapphire scales, the fish appeared. With a fishy smirk he granted Ragnar's wish.

Back at the new mansion the peddler appeared. In his cart was everything you might need for the party of the year. "Already paid for," said the peddler, tipping his hat.

When Ragnar came home, there were three hundred people on the front lawn. The orchestra played *The Waltz of the Midnight Sun.*

Ulla, in a festive gown with silver buckles on her shoes, danced with the old king of Norway.

Ragnar ate two curried shrimp puffs and went to bed.

In the morning Ulla said, "I danced with the king."

"I saw you," said Ragnar.

"He is a hundred years old," said Ulla. "He has no wife or children. Norway needs a young queen to rule when he is gone. Ask the fish, Ragnar. Oh, tell the fish I just need this one last thing and you will never have to go out in the boat to make a living in the hot sun or the cold wind again."

Ragnar rolled over in bed. "I think you've been bitten by the yellow-winged envy bug!" he grunted and went back to sleep.

For seven days Ulla badgered and bothered Ragnar, until one night he couldn't stand it any longer. He took the boat out in the moonlight for some peace and quiet. For many hours Ragnar rested on the gentle rolling swells and breathed in the warm and salty west wind.

"I can't stay here forever," he said to himself. "But I don't want to go home either. What should I do?" he asked the deep dark sea.

A pair of ruby lips blew bubbles at him from the foamy crest of a wave. "What is it now?" the fish asked.

"My wife says she needs to be queen of Norway," said Ragnar.

"Oh, I can't do that," said the fish, blinking his emerald eyes. "A good queen must think of other people all the time. Ulla would think only of herself."

Ragnar sailed home. "The fish says no," he told Ulla.

"Now we will never be happy," moaned Ulla.

"I'll tell you what," said Ragnar. "It would make *me* happy to listen to the sound of the gulls dropping their clams on the rocks beside the Torva Fjord."

Ragnar and Ulla took a walk by the shore of the Torva Fjord. When they heard the mewing of the gulls and the spattering of the clamshells, Ulla found herself humming one of her old songs.

At last they came to the front steps of their cottage. Ulla sighed.
"I think it would make me happy," she said, "to say hello to my petunias."
"It would make me happy," said Ragnar, "to eat a slice of your cloud-
berry cake and see you smile at me over the candle flames once again."

So Ragnar and Ulla resumed their old life. They were happy with no more than the taste of homemade bread and the smell of the west wind.

After a year and an evening had passed, there was a knock on the door.

"Don't answer it!" said Ragnar.

"It's your old friend, the peddler!" said a familiar voice.

The peddler's cart was filled with silver pots, velvet pillows, and expensive spices.

"We don't need anything," said Ulla.

Purring from the cart was a stray kitten with emerald eyes and ruby red lips.

"But that kitten needs us," said Ragnar.
"Already paid for!" said the peddler.